D1411297

STARR AND HER FAMILY HOST A FEAST

by Sahar Sabati

illustrated by Nelli Newport

To my dearly loved daughter,
our thoughtful and hardworking cohost.

Starr was especially excited to go home from school today because her family was hosting a Feast. Mom opened the door with a big smile.

After giving her a tight hug, she sent Starr to her room to change. "Be quick, we have a lot to prepare!"

Starr changed into a nice skirt and top she wore only for special occasions.

She then went to the kitchen. She knew her Feast responsibilities well. First, she wiped the dining room table with a big, wet cloth. She then took out a tablecloth and spread it carefully on the table, smoothing it out until it was completely straight.

She carefully laid out forks, knives, and spoons beside the pile of plates. She then arranged napkins beside the plates and lined the glasses and cups.

Her parents brought out trays and bowls filled with cookies and nuts that didn't need to stay in the fridge. It was hard not to eat anything!

When Starr and her parents were finished with their tasks, she went to the kitchen to eat dinner. Her Dad said: "Head up," then tucked a napkin into the collar of her shirt.

She was too big for a bib, but she was wearing her nice clothes, after all!

They had just finished washing their dinner dishes when the doorbell rang.

Starr was in charge of greeting everyone as they came in.
She showed them where they could put their shoes, place
their bags, and hang their coats. She then showed them
into the living room, where her parents would welcome them.

First came the Naraghi family.

"Alláh-u-Abhá, dear friends," Starr politely said to
Mr. and Mrs. Naraghi. She then grinned at their twin
daughters. "Hi, Sahba! Hi, Mahsa!"

The two of them grinned back at Starr, and together,
said: "Hi Starr!"

Someone else knocked at the door! Starr opened it, and in came the Andersons.

"Hello, Mr. and Mrs. Anderson. Come in, please," she said.

Before she could close the door, she noticed that the Bourgeois family was climbing up the stairs to the house. "Alláh-u-Abhá," she said.

She smiled up at the little baby Mr. Bourgeois was holding. He was so small! Starr wanted to play with him, but more people were already heading towards the door.

A minute before Feast was set to start, Mom came to get Starr; they slipped into the living room and, right after they had been seated, Feast began with the chairperson saying, as always: "Dear friends, welcome to the Feast!"

Starr loved the first part of Feast. Sometimes, people would chant prayers. Other times, everyone would sing prayers together. Tonight, even Starr joined in: "God is sufficient unto me; He verily is the All-sufficing! In Him let the trusting trust."

After a round of prayers, a few people would read short
sections from the Writings of Bahá'u'lláh, The Báb,
and 'Abdu'l-Bahá; her parents
played soft, relaxing music
in the background.

At their own home,
the Naraghis would light
candles, while the Andersons
had a bronze bowl one of them would rub
with a big stick to make it hum. It was very peaceful...

But Starr had a tough time
with the whole sitting
still thing.

It was really hard to not move around or open her eyes!

She thought she was going to burst when someone said:
"Thank you very much, dear friends, for the beautiful prayers."
This meant that the devotional part were over and the
consultative part was beginning!

Starr was relieved; it meant she could finally move. The first thing she did was to tuck her feet under her legs and move a little, quietly and discreetly, so she wouldn't disturb anyone.

During the consultative part, letters with advice on how to make their community better were read. Everyone then consulted about how to put the advice into practice.

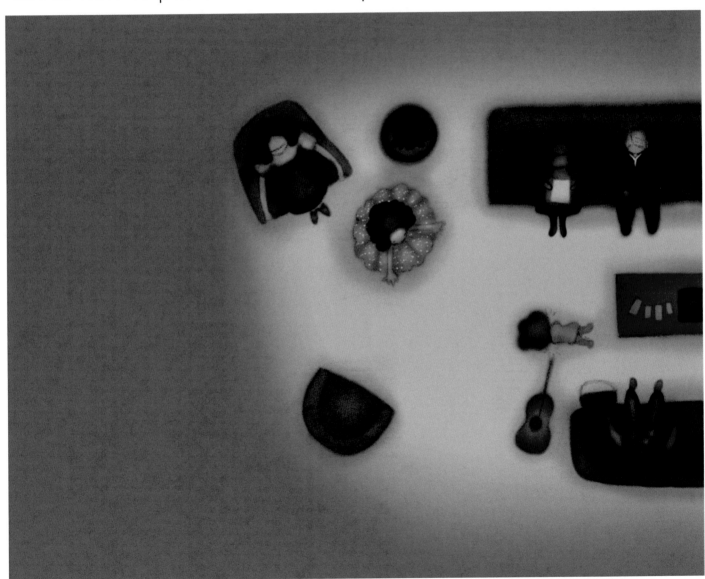

Mom and Dad encouraged her to share her ideas, but for now, Starr just listened. It was interesting, even if she didn't quite understand everything that was going on.

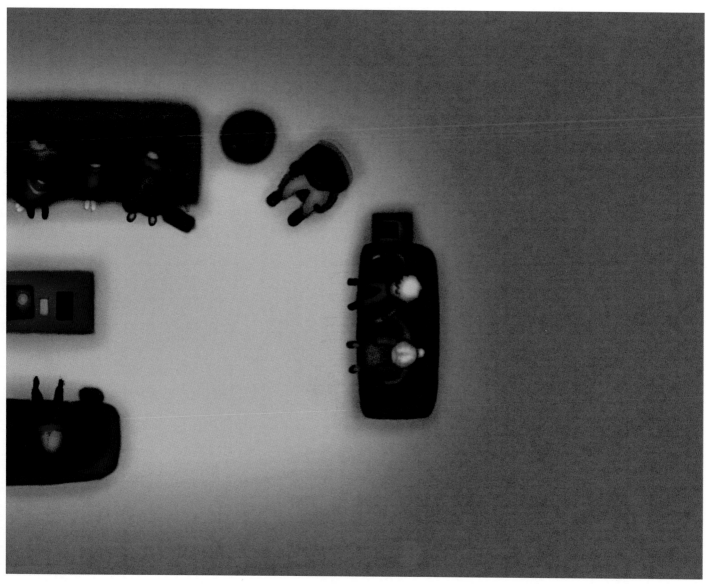

The consultative portion ended with a short prayer,
and everyone headed towards the dining room.
It was Starr's responsibility hand out
plates to each of their guests.

Afterwards, she would go to the kitchen and help her Mom
take out trays of vegetables and bowls of fruit
from the fridge out to the dining room.

The social portion was so much fun! Sometimes, people would sing; other times, they would bring out books and read portions of them out loud.

Once, someone decided to teach everyone a dance from their native country. Whatever happened, there was always a lot of laughter.

Starr was starting to get tired; she had some snacks, spent some time with her friends, then helped a little with the clean-up as people started to leave.

Slowly, the living room, dining room, and kitchen were back into their normal state of order and cleanliness.

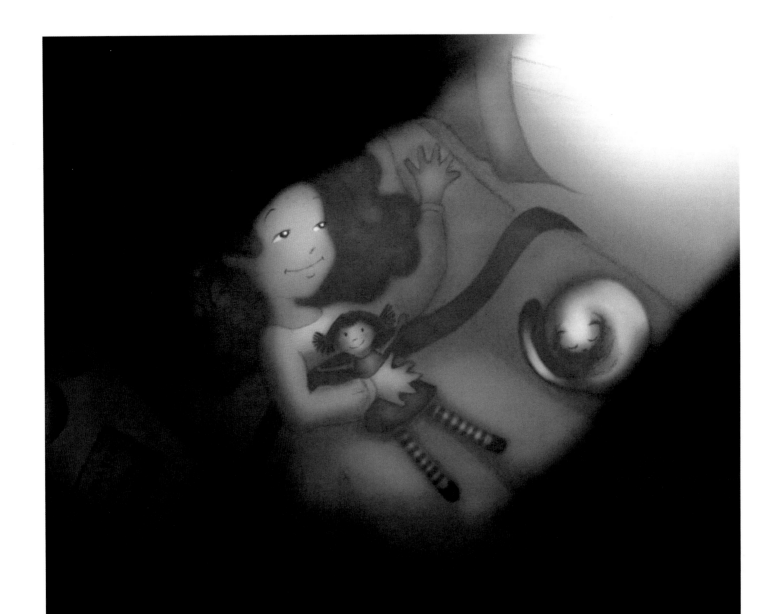

Starr could barely make it through her own prayers that night!
She had worked really hard to host Feast with her parents
from setup to cleanup, and it was way past her bedtime.

She was probably going to be tired at school tomorrow, but it was worth it. She smiled as she closed her eyes; she was looking forward to doing hosting Feast again!

Made in the USA
Monee, IL
07 November 2020

46480268R00021